NICOLETTE

OTHER BOOKS BY ROBERT ZEND

From Zero To One (Sono Nis Press, 1973)

My Friend Jerónimo (Omnibooks, 1981)

Arbormundi (blewointmentpress, 1982)

Beyond Labels (Hounslow Press, 1982)

Oāb (Exile, Volume 1, 1983; Volume 2, 1985)

The Three Roberts: Premiere Performance (HMS Press, 1984)

The Three Roberts: On Love (Dreadnaught, 1984)

The Three Roberts: On Childhood (Moonstone, 1985)

Versek, képversek (Atelier hongrois, 1988)

Daymares (Cacanadadada Press, 1991)

Hazám törve kettővel (Omnibooks, 1991)

Fából vaskarikatúrák (Magyar Világ Kiadó, 1993)

NICOLETTE

a novel novel

by

Robert Zend

CACANADADADA

NICOLETTE
Copyright © 1993 Janine Zend

CACANADADADA PRESS LTD.
3350 West 21st Avenue
Vancouver, B.C. Canada
V6S 1G7

Set in Galliard 10½ on 16
Typesetting: The Typeworks, Vancouver, B.C.
Printing: Hignell Printing, Winnipeg, Manitoba
Cover Photo: Albert Kish
Cover Design: Cecilia Jang

The publisher wishes to thank the Canada Council and the British Columbia Cultural Services Branch for their generous financial assistance.

CANADIAN CATALOGUING IN PUBLICATION DATA

Zend, Robert.
    Nicolette

    ISBN 0-921870-23-1

    I. Title.
PS8599.E52N5   1993   C811'.54   C93-091028-1
PR9199.3.Z45N5   1993

ACKNOWLEDGEMENTS

Nicolette was written in Hungarian by Robert Zend in 1976 and translated into English by the author.

Advice and assistance from Oliver Botár, Barry Callaghan, Aniko Zend-Gabori and Natalie Zend are gratefully acknowledged.

WARNING

THIS BOOK IS DEFINITELY A ONE-SHOT
EXPERIENCE. DO NOT START READING IT UNLESS
YOU HAVE AT LEAST ONE UNDISTURBED HOUR
FROM THIS MINUTE ON.

CHAPTERS FROM
AN UNWRITTEN NOVEL

• 2 7 •

Semi-darkness. The curtain is half-drawn. The moon shines through the top square of the window-pane. Silence in the garden. The surrounding houses are in utter darkness. Beyond them, Firenze sleeps. The walnut tree also sleeps in the garden.

My eyes are closed. I am on my back. My right hand rests on Nicolette's pudenda. She too is lying on her back. We have been lying like this for hours. Hours ago we stormed under, above, around each other, gentle kisses, fierce bites. Now we are resting.

Sometimes we are half-asleep. When we are awake, my hand wanders to her breasts, her loins, her knees. Debussy experimenting with piano keys, up to her hardening nipples, then back down, the swing of a pendulum, steadily, freely. Nicolette sighs, then sighs again, her face in the moonlight, as my gaze comes to rest on her like a gull on a rock. Her mouth seems to smile but doesn't smile, it sighs, oh . . . her eyes turn up and she turns her face to the left, and we are two parallel bodies with heads turned toward each other and four eyes but only two gazes that lock in a single link of a chain. Her lips open slowly, they call, shining, and my head moves, her head moves, my hand under her nape pulling her toward me, her hand on my hip pulling me toward her, mouth to mouth . . . and I wake up.

My pillow is damp, warm. I turn on my back. My wife breathes heavily and prattles in her sleep. "Getthe I tolyou ciffo . . ." silence, and then again more loudly, "Iwant get the Isaid oh Y'don't on plea . . ."

I look at the round alarm clock. It sits beside my wife on the bedside table. Its face is phosphorescent: five minutes to five, I slip soundlessly from the bed.

In the bathroom I raise the lid of the toilet. This would be the time to get dressed, to pull on a shirt, trousers, socks, shoes, jacket, to get money from the top drawer of the desk. Then the overcoat. All I want is to get away while Margit is still asleep. I insert the key softly so she doesn't wake up. Down the stairs on the double to the street, a taxi is rolling by, I signal, it brakes. When is the next plane to Florence? Hurry, the stewardess is closing the door. Hallo, here I am. I smile at her, she smiles back, seat G-6 near the window, and the engine surges, the earth slips backward and sinks away. Green meadows run up the left side-window while the right side-window is filled with clouds. Then the plane breaks through the clouds, revolving the earth below. I look down upon the clouds. They look the same from above and below, but instead of blue sky, now the dark earth hovers behind them. Then the earth disappears and the green ocean moves slowly back beneath us while the humming ma-chine remains majestically stationary: the centre of the world. Underneath, the waters are blown by the powerful engines to rotate backward, to rotate westward until the zigzagging shoreline of Europe arrives below us. Towns, fields, villages, mountains, valleys, lakes, highways, rivers in an endless procession, and a golden stripe signals the dawn. Nicolette. Towns, fields, villages, mountains, the sky turns from yellow to white. Nicolette. There had been a frontier between us, a big fat frontier consisting of a hundred rivers, a hundred mountains, millions and millions of tons of ocean, millions and millions of tons of air. But now the frontier is thinning and the body in which I am enclosed flies toward the body in which you are enclosed and these two bodies live, burst into flame, moan with pleasure when there is no frontier between them, and writhe with pain and whimper when they are apart. Nicolette. You are there among the houses of Firenze, the big fat frontier is thinning, my ears ache, the plane brakes, the engine roars, the wheels touch ground, the noise increases and suddenly stops. Taxi! Through the sleeping streets of Firenze. Black towers against the dark blue sky. The gate is open, I advance soundlessly across the garden to the old walnut tree, and enter silently through the window, dropping my clothes on the floor. Lightly, like a cat, I lower my body on the bed, to Nicolette's left where there is an empty place for me, and lift my right hand and place it delicately lest she wake, on her inner thigh.

Semi-darkness. The curtain is half-drawn. The full moon shines through the top square of the window-pane. Silence in the garden. The surrounding houses are in utter darkness. Beyond them, Firenze sleeps. The walnut tree also sleeps in the garden. It doesn't rustle.

My eyes are closed. I am lying on my back. My right hand is on Nicolette's quim. She is lying on her back. We have been like this for hours.

The bed creaks. Margit totters, still drunk with her sleep, to the bathroom. "—Listen—I had such an awful dream. You ran away in the night and left me forever, flew somewhere in Europe, and I ran up and down the street but couldn't find you anywhere. It seemed too real and I'm so happy you're here! When I woke I put out my hand, and you weren't there. I thought the dream was true." She rests her head on my shoulder.

I stroke her hair, take her hand, and gently pull her back, but she gently pushes me out of the bathroom. "—Since I am here, anyway—" and smiles at me.

Traces of the dream-kiss are damp on my pillow. I try to conjure Nicolette on my right, but see only the sheet and blanket. I try to sense the warmth of Nicolette's loins but my fingers touch only the blanket. I try to see her face shining with unearthly delight, but instead I see the phosphorescent white of a round clock-animal. Four minutes to five.

Toronto, January 12, 1972

• 2 4 •

You ache
like an arm
cut off at the shoulder

•24•

You ache
like an arm
cut off

• 2 4 •

Like an arm
cut off at the shoulder
you ache

• 2 4 •

You ache
like an arm cut off at the shoulder
continuing to ache

• 2 4 •

You ache
like an arm left on the battlefield
continues to ache

• 2 4 •

Nicolette,
like an arm left on the battlefield
you continue to ache

• 2 9 •

I am writing you now, Nicolette, a report of what hasn't happened. I am writing this letter because, at last, I have the time, because I don't have to sit hunched over my desk, because at last I have the time, because I am driving my car and have twenty minutes to write you this letter. I am writing, Nicolette, to Firenze, and I repeat the sentence again and again, caressing every word, I AM WRITING YOU NOW, NICOLETTE, TO FIRENZE, for I treasure every word of this sentence. I love the word LETTER because it links me with you. I love the word WRITING because it is hard and strong and rough and dense. WRITING, like the wool of a sheep being combed, and the horn comb sparks on the skin; I am writing you

NOW, I shall insert NOW, because I love that word as I love life and life is a series of Nows, and when I hear the word NOW I always remember that NOW of days gone by. Nows so truly, so searingly Now and you were intertwined with that Now and for you I was the Now and for me your voice was the Now and the round gestures of your hands were the Now and the taste of your kiss was the Now; I am writing TO YOU. I love these words, too, because they are members of a family of words whose every member I love (a drunk almost stepped in front of the car: they won't even let me write here) and the names of the members are you, with you, by you, to you, for you, on you, beside you, below you, above you, around you . . . oh, I am wrong. I don't love every member in that family, there are some I hate, some who make me shudder, like from you, without you . . . and NICOLETTE, how I love your name because it is like you, the NI like your impish, girlish, glittering laughter, the CO like your thick black hair and the LETTE, playful and charming like your smile or the self-revealing blaze of your eyes, and oh, FIRENZE, the town, our mute witness, our enfolding environment, our warmly rocking, pampering bed, yes. I am writing you a letter now, Nicolette, to Firenze, and I write in haste because I don't know how much longer you will be there (I ran a traffic light!), not for months, that much I know, but for weeks, perhaps, and then you'll go back and everything will be over, or will begin anew, it depends on you, it depends only on me, on you and me, on YouandI, this mysterious new being which sprang from our coupling and yet isn't our child, but our relationship, ourselves, each other_____

_____

I had to interrupt my letter-writing because I arrived at my office and I cannot write to you to Firenze because I am sitting behind a desk and there are papers in front of me and pencils and pens, and in a situation like this one cannot write. Someone asked for a lift in my car, a friend, because the mornings here are very cold, and I had to suspend writing to you because we were talking, only once was I able to address a few words to you, teaching you how to drive: look, when you make a turn you have to keep both hands on the steering wheel, and don't cut the corner, and you leaned against me and your voice was soft in my ear, of course I understand, you said, but then my friend began to talk and I shrugged, what can I do, and you gave me a conspiratorial look, never mind.

Now I am working alone in my office, it is eleven o'clock, almost noon, I am hungry, but there is something I want to show you, I know you are interested in my work, look, this is where you thread in the film, and here's the sound track, see? Would you like a try? Not now. It's all right. Here is where we cut the film, see? The motion is halved but in the next roll we'll find the continuity, only from a different angle. What shall I show you now? _____

_____

_____

No, don't sit there. Not behind me. At this studio I am the boss. I throw out even the President, but you are something else again, sharing my chair, so don't worry about anything. What makes you laugh? That they can't see you? It's funny but true. How can they see you, if you are in Firenze? Do you want to embarrass me? Not on your sweet life!

She is good, that woman, isn't she? What? Edith, kindly repeat that last sentence, more slowly, in a deeper voice. Yes, she's sixty-two. Yes, I agree she's a nice person. And she speaks beautifully.

_____

_____ In the restaurant I steal looks at you, she doesn't understand why I don't look at her. You wink at me, Edith says there is only one law: I. The first person singular. Do you agree? So do I. But Edith, in certain situations I am a coward. I'll give you an example. This isn't a real case but an imaginary one. I've just invented it. See: I have a wife, Margit, and she loves me. And I love her, too. Now then. Let's suppose that a month ago I went away on business. Let's say I went to the Riviera. To Nice. There, I met a young woman (don't fret, Nicolette). She is twenty-two and her name is Tamara. She's got Russian blood. Blond, full-lipped, full-busted, that's all I knew about her. And we fell in love. She came up to my room. We lay on the bed. I noticed a letter that had fallen out of her pocketbook. Krasnejev. The name of my best friend, Vladimir Krasnejev, the painter, my closest friend, and I haven't seen him for five years, but they said he married a woman forty years younger. I rose from the bed. Tamara pulled me back. I can't, I said, it's impossible! Be quiet and listen, Tamara said. He knows. How can he know! I cried. Did you write him about me? He doesn't know about you. He knows I have lovers. Sex no longer interests him. And I need it. We have an agreement. I kissed her. I put my arms around her. But I couldn't make love to her. There is something . . . something . . . I said. I just can't do it. A thousand unknown lovers are nothing, but me, his best friend?

She said: as Vladimir's wife I agree with you, but don't make love to Vladimir's wife, make love to me because you love me and I love you. See me. And I saw Tamara. And Vladimir's face, which had been watching anxiously, disappeared and never reappeared while we were together, but that's only one side of the coin, Edith, the other is Margit, whom I love. What'll I do?

Edith gives me an ironic look. She doesn't agree. I shrug. Tomorrow, I do this. The day after, I do that. In the evening, Margit waits for me.

And you, Nicolette, you sit there on that empty chair looking at me contemptuously and at Edith with affection.

It's a fruitless discussion. Let's stop it. And once more I drop into bed late at night next to Margit. She is asleep and doesn't wake up ——————————————————————————————

_____

_____

_____

_____

_____

_____ Next morning. The letter continues. I am going away. I am going to New York alone. You are sitting next to me. You don't speak about Edith. You look at me sideways but we don't talk.

In New York I meet Birabeau again. I attend the first performance of his new symphony. It is a fantastic success. Afterwards, he invites me. He asks about you. It feels good to talk about you. He says neither yes nor no. He doesn't agree or disagree. He just asks. And understands. He obviously knows that it is up to me.

You hang on his every word. You like Birabeau very much. A pity you aren't here. A pity he doesn't know you. You'd like Birabeau very much. And you'd love his music. _____

_____

_____

____ Here I lie on the double bed in my hotel. The letter is writing itself non-stop. I have been writing it long before I started writing, and I shall continue writing it long after I have finished writing. A letter without end. The television is on, but I don't see the picture and don't hear the sound. You are lying next to me and you are stroking my hair. Nicolette. I put out the light. It is dark. And before I fall asleep, in that one second before I sink into the humming-darkness, in that second of semi-darkness, I seal the envelope and post this letter. I don't know what post box swallows it, whether it is grey or blue, whether it is attached to a house wall or standing on four legs. I don't know whether it is American, Italian or Russian. All I know is that it has an oblong, wide mouth, but the rest of it disappears in the mist. It isn't in a street, it isn't on a wall, there are no people around it, only emptiness. There is a black void, and in the centre of that void a wide, oblong mouth. I see my white hand, but not myself, as it holds the sealed envelope, raises it slowly to the oblong mouth and throws it in, then the letter disappears and with it the letter-box and my white hand and me for seven or eight hours. I cease knowing about myself and Edith and Birabeau and perhaps I even cease knowing about you for seven or eight hours, but in the morning I shall wake as I always wake: Nicolette and the letter. Do you hover near all night?

I don't know. I don't know anything . . . . Nicolette
I sleep. I don't exist. I don't remember. . . . . N i c o l e t t e
There is nothing. Nothing. Nothing . . . . N i c o l e t t e
Only I. I. I. . . . . N i c o l e t t e
Not even I. . . . . N i c o l e t t e
Only am. Am. Am. . . . . N i c o l e t t e
Am without I. . . . . N i c o l e t t e
. . . . N i c o l e t t e
. . . . N i c o l e t t e

• — 1 •

The little man's face is stubbornly pentagonal, his nose is crooked, his hair is black. When I sit, he sits opposite me, when I stand, he stands opposite me, when I walk he walks toward me, we never run into each other but he is always walking toward me as if his walking toward me were happening on a screen in front of me; and when I lie on my bed he stands at the foot and stares at me.

I haven't been able to discover how this little man looks on the inside. At times it seems as if his black button-eyes are sparkling with the brilliance of genius, and at other times they seem blank and stony. At times I feel that he is like a cooling ointment and more often I believe that he is an executioner, and enjoys his job.

This little man doesn't behave as if he were his own master but as if he had been sent by someone, some distant lord or a natural law that invented this little man in order to take shape in him, inhabit him. Below his thick black hair, above his forehead, I imagine two little horns; perhaps they are curls in his hair or protrusions from his forehead, I don't know. The little man's vocabulary consists of two words, or three, and he looks at me with interest, with indifference, sometimes bored, sometimes disgusted, while at times he seems excited and his gaze is an inspiration, as if he were saying: "Talk . . . go ahead . . . talk!" And I talk and his reply is always the same:

—Forget her.

Sometimes like this, threateningly, commandingly:

—Forget her!

Sometimes like this, softly, comfortingly:

—Forget her . . .

I'd need fifty years to write down everything I have to say. I have only twenty left. What'll I do about those thirty years? What'll I do with all the material I've no time to write down?

—Forget it.

I also want to paint in oil and pastel because I am haunted by pictures that ask to be painted. But now I have neither the money nor the time. How could I . . .

—Forget it.

I should like to investigate the relationship between race and individual. I want to carry out foetus experiments in a laboratory. I would have to purchase some five hundred books for it, buy instruments, invent new instruments. And I'd require about fifteen years to do this exclusively . . .

—Forget it.

This life is not enough for me, I want several lives. It's highly unsatisfactory, existing in only one copy, because one is limited by time. Several lives, or several thousand years . . .

—Forget it.

I am fascinated by the infinite in whose one, tiny fraction I exist. How can I live if I don't know of what I am a part? If there is a purpose, I should work for it, but I don't know what the purpose is. And if there is no purpose, it would allow me to be irresponsible, but I don't know what responsibility I'd be irresponsible in relation to . . .

—Forget it.

Will everything petrify into nothingness when my heart stops? Does the past in which I moved and on which I trod, trying to leave my mark, become as if it had never been? Or does my memory survive, and does the continuity which was called "I" move into a new body? Or will a new dimension open before me, from which all this will appear flat as the paper I am now writing on? What will happen when my seconds run out?

—Forget it.

I am happy, I am so happy, I want to remain happy forever . . .

—Forget it.

I suffer, I am tormented, sharp teeth tear the invisible matter of my soul, how long . . .

—Forget it.

I want to love Nicolette, be with her always, move into her orbit, hold her hand and gaze into her eyes. I'll never forget her. What'll I do with Nicolette?

—Forget her.

I adore life! The simple and the unfathomable. I delight in solving mysteries but I also adore running into walls. I get the keenest pleasure because everything is equivocal and even ambiguity is ambiguous, because deep down it is unequivocal. I adore life!

—Forget it.

· 3 0 ·

Anastasius, the artist (it's a pseudonym, of course; I am speaking of myself), was, to put it mildly, a schizophrenic. His illness progressed silently in the labyrinthine, dark corridors of his heart.

Now, if a schizophrenic happens to split into two personalities, one of which wants to live, for instance, in Hungary as a writer, and the other, let us say, in Toronto as a film director, the schizophrenic will yield to one of his two desires and live, let us say, in Toronto, but in Toronto he will come into conflict with himself because he wants to live in Budapest as well, as a writer. If it so happens that the schizophrenic is a writer, then he will act out his schizophrenia on paper, which is generally called literature and which saves the schizophrenic from being shut up in a lunatic asylum, instead of which he will be accepted as a normal abnormal (in public parlance, an artist).

In Anastasius' case (which, as we shall see, had a fateful influence on the further history of mankind) the schizophrenia was a public danger because Anastasius' personality split down the middle not only symbolically but in fact. He split into two Anastasiuses. One of them went off to Toronto to direct films, the other to Budapest to write. Thus, there was no cause for either to come into conflict with himself.

This, however, was only the beginning. Anastasius was a philanderer and, while living with his nice wife, fell in love with a French girl who in turn fell in love with him because he, too, was nice, and opposites attract each other. But Anastasius loved his wife as well and couldn't choose. Nor was there any need for it. Another personality-split, and one of him married the French girl, avoiding a conflict with himself, not to speak of bigamy. So that there should be no misunderstanding, this happened to the Toronto Anastasius.

At the same time, the writer Anastasius who lived in Budapest and was also married, fell in love with a Hungarian girl, split down the middle and married her as well, also without committing bigamy. By then, four Anastasiuses existed in the world, a film director and a radio director in Toronto, a writer and a poet in Budapest.

Anastasius was not only a philanderer of catholic tastes but also gifted and versatile. While he existed in one copy only, lack of time prevented him from being, at the same time, a painter, sculptor, pianist, composer, embryologist, botanist, gardener, decorator and economist. Now, however, as his illness gained ground, time was no longer a consideration. For, as we know, a pianist has to practise ten hours a day which doesn't allow four hours for writing, eight hours for experimentation, spending the day in the garden, painting in the mountains, etc., etc.

But things became more and more involved. The Anastasius who lived in Toronto and was the French girl's husband and radio director, one day split into two and became an Italian professor as well, while the Anastasius who lived with the nice wife and was a film director, also split and became a sculptor as well. The Budapest-Anastasius also multiplied by fission, the Anastasius husband-of-the-first-wife became a pianist while the other half remained a writer. The Anastasius husband-of-the-new-girl turned into a classical philologist while his other half remained a poet and continued spending his days at the café. Naturally, the four wives were somewhat surprised, at first, when each had two husbands come home to dinner in the evening, but this situation was soon solved in various ways. The poet-Anastasius challenged the classical philologist Anastasius to a duel and killed him. The pianist Anastasius fell in love with a Canadian tourist and emigrated to Canada, thus the writer Anastasius remained alone in Budapest. The Italian professor and the radio director in Canada remained with the original wife and both gave maintenance money to the French wife who was delighted with the two husbands and the double alimony because she was sensual and greedy. The wife of the sculptor and film director Anastasiuses couldn't put up with two husbands and kicked them both out but they didn't mourn for long and split into two . . .

It would be far too complicated to follow the involved careers of our several Anastasiuses beyond this point. It suffices to say that the Anastasiuses began to play an increasingly important part in the life of society and, gradually, began to crowd out all others. Naturally, they all supported each other and when an Anastasius was called upon to choose between an Anastasius and someone else, it is clear that, due to human weakness . . .

They began to rule the world's love-life. They travelled a great deal and every trip ended in a new marriage. They exiled more and more husbands and fathers from their homes and turned them into bachelors by seducing their wives...the number of jobless and homeless grew to unheard-of proportions.

The spread of the illness went hand in hand with the acceleration of its progression. The Anastasiuses reached crossroads almost every moment of their lives. It frequently occurred that when an Anastasius couldn't choose between his two favourite dishes in a restaurant, there were suddenly two Anastasiuses, each ordering one of the favourite dishes. Or, when an Anastasius had to decide whether to go to the theatre or meet a girl, he went to both places at the same time. Thus, every alternative ended in two Anastasiuses, as a result of which there were no inner conflicts but there were new marriages and new jobs. Before long, there was a population explosion of Anastasiuses, and who could resist such dynamism, such elementary force? The Anastasiuses were healthy, enthusiastic, uninhibited, virile, without the slightest trace of hesitation or neurosis. They were possessed by an inner calm, while non-Anastasius mankind didn't have a chance; they indulged in mass suicide, died of starvation, or went mad from hopeless love.

It didn't take long before mankind was made up of three billion Anastasiuses (which, of course, is a pseudonym for myself). (And this story now comes to a dead-end because I have a dilemma and cannot make up my mind.)

• 0 •

It is possible that this will fall into somebody's hands. It is possible that, one day, it will be published. I couldn't care less.

It is possible that even I won't like it tomorrow. But just now, I don't care.

I am not writing it for people to like. I don't care about anyone else. Whether that "anyone" is another human being, the reading public, myself tomorrow, or posterity.

"He is trying to be original, that's why he writes his chapters haphazardly instead of consecutively. First 27, then a series of 24s, then 29, then minus 1, and then a short story. This man must want people to think he's crazy! Or clever!"

Who cares? I know why I write this way. It is very simple. I'm not trying to be original and I'm not crazy. They are crazy. They, who place everything in little boxes and glue masks to their faces and insist others do the same. They, who mould others in their own image. Let them leave me in peace.

I ruminate. In the recent past. I ruminate because the soul remembers the way a cow ruminates. Things don't come back to me in an orderly order. But like this: this is what happened on Friday, this is taking place today, and then there was Wednesday and Tuesday. I recall nothing about Thursday. Is that a crime?

Wouldn't I create real chaos if I chronologically set out sections of time-transformed-into-memory which has already structured itself independently of chronology? I remain true to reality only if my tortuous ruminations are tortuously numbered.

Why begin with 27? I don't know. Intuitively. More or less it would have been the 27th chapter had I come chronologically. And the next, the 24th, because it happened somewhat earlier. The 29th happened a short time after the 27th but I left something out, and the "minus one" is something I felt for a long time, long before I met Nicolette, and what I am writing now is the introduction, which is why it is 0. If I followed the objective sequence of events I would falsify the chronology of my subjective creation. This way is closer to the truth.

Nicolette will understand. Nicolette won't believe I'm trying to be original. Or clever.

Immortality? Posterity? Others? What do I care?

I am writing a message to Nicolette. Because she is far away and because she wants to know. Not what has happened, she knows that already, but what is now rippling within me.

Nobody, nothing exists. There is only Nicolette.

She is posterity. She is the present. She is the other.

She is I.

• 1 5 •

I am too old for you, I said to her.
It doesn't matter, she replied, it evens out.
What evens out, I asked, what do you mean?
I mean that I, on the other hand, am too young for you.

• 2 2 •

I cannot tell you, my dear lady, why I am sad. But try to imagine that I am travelling in a spaceship toward Pluto. And another spaceship is coming from Pluto. The two spaceships are destined to meet, their hulls touch as they pass each other in opposite directions, and as the hulls touch, doors open wider and wider, and widest when the two hulls are parallel, and then, as they move on, the doors become narrower and narrower. The whole thing lasts only minutes but during those minutes crates are shifted from ship to ship. Medicines in exchange for fuel. The doors close. I am a passenger. I am travelling to Pluto on official business. I shall return only in 450 years, by which time I'll be 45 years older. When the door opens I glimpse a face in the other ship the like of which I have never seen in the entire universe. It is the face of a girl and she, too, stares at me and I realize that for her too, I am the one. She, too, is travelling on official business to Mars and after that to the third moon of Saturn. She will return to Earth only in 973 years, by which time she will be 75 years old. There is no time for preliminaries, we begin to talk. By the time the door is fully open, we are kissing each other like mad. The door begins to close and now, gabbling, stammering, cutting into each other's words, we tell each other everything about ourselves, our childhood, our loves...

You ask me, dear lady, why I am sad?

(Darkness. Cheering. The sound of kissing. Happy New Year! Happy New Year!)

I am sad, dear lady, because that door is so narrow we can only hold hands. Then, our fingers begin to slide from each other's grasp...

This is why. Apart from that, Happy New Year! The same to me? Thank you.

· 2 0 ·

Nicolette, this is perfect happiness. To sit here with you in the car at two o'clock in the morning and talk. And half an hour ago, that was the perfect happiness. To lie in bed with you, to touch, to hold, to caress, to embrace, to pant, to bite. And three hours ago that was the perfect happiness. To sit in a cinema, to watch whatever it was and to know that you are there, next to me. When you speak to me, that is perfect. When you listen to me speaking, that is perfect. And when we are both silent, that is perfect. You and I together are perfection itself. YouandI is perfect. What do you think of that? YouandI. A good name for us, isn't it? I've never been so complete. So happy.

Yes, Nicolette, I've never been so unhappy. It is unbearable, the thought that we are puppets pulled by fate, or destiny, or heaven knows what. Because now, as we sit here in the car, we feel that we are free. Free to love, to kiss, to meet. It is not so. It's two o'clock in the morning and it is certain that in the next ten or fifteen minutes you will get out of this car. And it is certain that in the next hour or two I shall go home and fall asleep. And it is certain that we shall meet twice, or four times more, and then I'll leave and you'll stay here. We are free only in the or, in the ten or fifteen minutes, in the one or two hours, in the two or four meetings. Time flies.

I'd like to shout for help. Stop time! I want to stay here! I want to stay here, in this car, forever! With you, holding your hand, forever! Gaze at the Arno bridge in front of us, forever! At the darkly slumped mountain on the other side of the river on which David stands, never sleeping, never moving, forever! And to the right and left the ancient houses, broken-walled towers, forever! Forever, forever, here with you, in Firenze, now! I want to stay here! I want to stay here in this second! Here forever!

Help! But no voice replies and time rolls on, it rolls on even while I shout for help.

It is hopeless. What am I to do? The little dark man's reply is always the same. What shall we do? What can we do? We are shipwrecked in an ocean bordered by horizons—the tallest mast will soon be under water—where is the floating plank? Hold on, until—

Perhaps . . . yes . . . I know . . .

Kiss me!

• 2 1 •

A shadow
falls on the kiss:
on the now the future.

· 1 8 ·

Strange. Before it happened I had pangs of conscience because of Gaston. Afterwards they disappeared. Before it happened, you were taboo. Afterwards you were my lover. Until now, you were Gaston's wife. Now, you are you. Nicolette. You were born.

•50•

You want to become a poem, don't you Nicolette?
You want me to kill you
and carve a woman-rhyme from your two legs, man-rhyme
from your two arms,
rhythm from your impish laughter,
and adjective out of your navel,
an adverbial complement from the warmth of your body,
a verb out of your movements,
you want me to kill you not embrace you,
sing you rather than kiss you,
send you into the future, not a son;

you want to read me rather than see flame in my eye . . .
You'd rather be a poem, wouldn't you, Nicolette?

That is what you want,
that is what he wants,
the voice inside that ceaselessly speaks,
that petrifies my soaring words,
that flattens my body
on sheets of paper before it can decompose . . .

I struggle, pushing you away now, and now him:
I want to live and not to write.
I will not allow you to become a poem, I will not!
Just wait.
I'm on my way.

January 15, 1972

•49•

Were I to keep a diary of the thoughts
that fill my head,
it'd be monotonous,
for this is what I would write:

nicolettenicolettenicolettenicolettenicolettenicolettenicoletten
icolettenicolettenicolettenicolettenicolettenicolettenicoletteni
colettenicolettenicolettenicolettenicolettenicolettenicolettenic
olettenicolettenicolettenicolettenicolettenicolettenicolettenico
lettenicolettenicolettenicolettenicolettenicolettenicolettenicol
ettenicolettenicolettenicolettenicolettenicolettenicolettenicole
ttenicolettenicolettenicolettenicolettenicolettenicolettenicolet
tenicolettenicolettenicolettenicolettenicolettenicolettenicolett
enicolettenicolettenicolettenicolettenicolettenicolettenicolette

I ASK NICOLETTE	NICOLETTE ASKS ME
Do you love me?	N: Why do you love me?
N: Don't ask . . .	Because you are beautiful.
Do you love me?	N: Why do you love me?
N: I think so.	Because you are good.
Do you love me?	N: Why do you love me?
N: Yes.	Because you are clever.
Do you love me?	N: Why do you love me?
N: I love you.	Because you love me!
Do you love me?	N: Why do you love me?
N: I love you. Do you love me?	Because you are
I love you.	what you are!
I love you!	N: Why do you love me?
N: I love you!	Because you are!
I love you,	N: Why do you love me?
I love you,	Because
I love you,	I love
do you love me?	myself
N: I love you,	when I am
I love you,	with
I love you!	you!

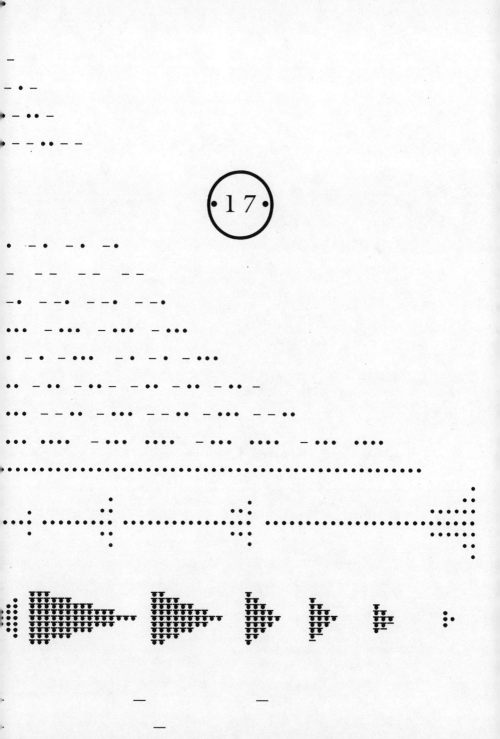

• 2 8 •

From sleep to wakefulness—
From wakefulness to sleep—
In vain—there's no escape.

• 2 8 •

The night is full with Nicolette—
The day is full with Nicolette—
To be asleep, to be awake, the same—

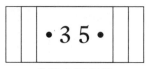

SURVEY

(To be able to continue)

−1. The little man. (Destiny, time, etc.)

  0. Direction for use. (Or introduction.)

1,2,3,4,5,6,7,8,9,10,11,12,13,14. . . . . . . unwritten, to be written.

15. In front of the hotel. (Too old—too young.)

16. Unwritten, to be written.

(17.) Lovemaking.

18. Afterwards about what was before.

19. Do you love me? Why do you love me?

20. Auto-monologue.

21. Echo of former.

22. New Year's Eve-party.

23. Unwritten, to be written.

24. Haiku. (After separation.) (Several attempts.)

25,26. Unwritten, to be written.

27. Dream, wakefulness, day-dream. (This is where the book began.)

28. Haiku. Summary of previous chapter.

29. Letter to Firenze.

30. Short story about Anastasius.

31,32,33,34,35,36,37,38,39,40,41,42,43,44,45,46,47,48, Unwritten. To be.

49. If-diary.

50. Becoming a poem.

  ∞. Unwritten. (The end is the beginning.)

I have to include this page as well because it is part of the process. Let it be 35. Why? Because it is half-way. (Nel mezzo del cammin . . .)

· 17 ·

Darkness. Curtain. Darkness. Moon. Two darknesses. Roomdarkness. Eyeliddarkness. Mouth. Forehead. Cheek. Kiss. Kiss. Warm. Soft. Hard. Flexible. Flesh. Warm. Soft. Moon. Wet. Flesh. Eye. Looks. Laughs. Oh. Elbow. Arm. Upperarm. Handclutch. Neck. Slender. Gazelle. Gripping. Back. Waist. Bottom. Thigh. Kiss. Long. Sigh. Eyelidkiss. Mouthkiss. Cheekkiss. Neckkiss. Breastkiss. Leftbreast. Long. Sigh. Oh. Oh. Oh. Rightbreast. Oh. Turnheraround. Leftbreastgrasp. Napekiss. Backkiss. Spinekiss. Long. Downwardkiss. Leftbottomkiss. Sheonherstomach. Ionherback. Leftbreastfondling. Rightbreastfondling. Oh. Oh. Downwardkiss. Thighkiss. Innerthighkiss. Leftinnerthighkiss. Rightinnerthighkiss.

Abovekneekiss. Leftright. Rightleft. Legkiss. Footkiss. Toekiss. Giggles. Legupwardkiss. Kneekiss. Bellykiss. Oh. Sigh. Leftbreastsuck. Oh. Leftbreastgrasp. Rightbreastsuck. Ah. Waistembrace. Oh. Seething. Kiss. Tongue. Tongueredtaste. Neckbite. Seething. Shoulderbite. Lipbite. Oh. Trumpet. Waistembrace. Oh. Waistclasp. No. Attack. No. No. Oh. Convulsion. Kneelifting. Attack. Orchestra. Trumpet. You. Sogoodsogood. You. Oh. Neverbefore. Gate. Walls. Gate. Walls. Eye. Soft. Eyelid. Eye. Eyelid. Sea. Storm. Wavecrest. Hurricane. Waves. Gulls. Wavetowers. Storm. Downpour. Hurricane. Tunnel. Skate. Running. Back. There. Lipbite. Back. There. Liptear. Pulsating. Ocean. Hurricane. Roaring. Trumpets. Army. Waterfall. Oh. Mighty. Giant. Pulsating. Whirlpool. Now. Now. Now. Now. Now. Now. Ohohohohohoh. Andnow. Ah. Ah. Andnow. Aaaah. Iam. Youare. Ah. Iare. Youam. YouI. Is. YouandI. Is. Nothing. Isn't. OnlyYouandI. Now. Thunder. Lightning. Downpour. Waterfall. Unutterable. Unutterable. More. Stillmore. Yes. Yes. Ah. Kiss. Flesh. Mouth. Eye. Moon. Curtain. Darkness. Sigh. Cheek. Eye. Kiss. Moon. Darkness.

• 4 7 •

He emerged
created someone to take his place
and burst.

January 22, 1972

The difference between the father and the artist is that the former creates someone, the latter something to take his place.

• 4 7 •

He emerged
created something to take his place
and burst.

January 22, 1972

Ibid. The difference between the father and the artist is that the former creates someone, the latter something—

• 31 •

Not Tamara, of course, but Nicolette. And naturally not Vladimir, but Gaston. They are not Russian, but French. It wasn't at the last moment that the letter fell out of the handbag but I had to lie to Edith to give her a true picture. You can not only lie to everyone at the same time (art) to give them a true picture of reality but you can lie to individuals (speaking in their language) (I learned this, too, from Nicolette . . .). The other details, however, which I told Edith were true (almost).

Had I told Edith that I'd always known Tamara (Nicolette) was Gaston's (Vladimir's) wife, then she'd have felt (mistakenly) that I was the seducer. It was Tamara.

And if I had told Edith that Tamara (Nicolette) had always known I was Gaston's (Vladimir's) best friend, then she would have been under the impression (mistakenly) that the coquette Tamara was the seducer. It was I.

Actually, I lied to her about the letter which fell out of the handbag at the last moment. I could not talk about the mystical YouandI in the framework of a real story told chronologically. The YouandI took shape by progressive stages. The name was the last to be born. I read it the first time in Nicolette's letter but when I asked her about it (because I could not make out the word) she said that I had invented the name in the car. However, before it had a name, we knew that it existed. Since when did it exist? Since we first met, Nicolette and I. She was five years old. And I, twenty-five.

• 1 •

A study trip to Paris. To meet the subject of my new book, the legendary Gaston Debrières-Salis, the greatest living French painter. After the first hour, in spite of our twenty-year age difference, we feel that we are contemporaries, childhood friends. Only the first few minutes are tense. He is free. I am inhibited. Then, shyly, I bring out my manuscript and hand it to him. He reads it avidly and from time to time exclaims: *Incroyable!* By the time he puts the manuscript down he calls me by my first name.—What intuition! What intellect. You are the first who might teach even me something about myself. All the others . . . (he shrugs). You know, to be "great," it is not so simple as they imagine, down there. They praise me, but they misunderstand me. They praise me but they interpret me. You, however, express what I cannot express about myself, things I thought about this or that, word for word, formulated by myself. Tonight I shall take you to Goudrier, Arthur Goudrier, my friend, my critic, who "discovered" me. He, too, misunderstands me. You must meet him. Or, rather, he must meet you . . .

After dinner Goudrier took us to the nursery. Nicolette was in bed wearing a little pink nightdress. I greeted her, played with her, made her laugh. She was a little woman. When I left, she called me back from the door.— Where have you been until now?— she asked with sincere curiosity.— Everywhere— I replied.— I met your father only today.— And weren't you interested in me until today?— she asked, a little offended.— Well . . . I didn't even know you existed . . . She thought about it, then shrugged.— Let's not talk about what was. The important thing is that now you know.

· 5̶ · · 6 ·

Mon cher Robert,

    Thank you for your letter and forgive me for having waited three months to answer it. I am preparing an exhibition and haven't got a moment. I am working on the *chef d'oeuvre* of my life, my own Mona Lisa (with a new model). I hardly have any time because of the exhibition. I sent off Nicolette to Firenze for three months, even her presence disturbs me. You say that you are planning to visit Venice and Rome. If you have a little time, go and visit her. She is at the Excelsior. I think she would be delighted. We read your latest poems with great pleasure. You did things few have dared to do. If you come to Paris, visit me, but please, only after the 15th of March. I'll tell you more about Mona Lisa then. An embrace.

Gaston

· 1 5 ·

I opened the door for Nicolette.—Thank you—she said. I went around the car and sat in the driver's seat.—How did you like the concert?—It was wonderful—said Nicolette. Somehow, the conversation was slow to start. At other times, Nicolette never ceased prattling, smiling, but now she was quiet.—Shall I take you somewhere for a cup of coffee?—No.—A drink?—No.—You mean you want to go back to your hotel?—No . . . —whispered Nicolette dreamily. I frowned: neither back home, nor a drink . . . —Do you want to go and dance somewhere?—No.—In that case, where do you want to go? (Nicolette remained silent.) Nicolette, what is the matter with you?—I asked, but I already knew. I only pretended not to know because I hoped I was wrong. She looked at me and her eyes overflowed with tears. I stopped the car.—Nicolette, you are crying. Do you have bad news from Paris? (She shook her head.) Gaston? (She shrugged with irritation.) (Perhaps it would be better not to find out . . .) I'll take you to your hotel, all right? (She shook her head slowly, tears glittered in the corner of her eye but she smiled at me.)—Nicolette, tell me what you want!—Do you have to be told everything, you . . . you writer? (And she dropped her head on my shoulder and began to sob.) Suddenly, there was total confusion in my head. Gaston! Twenty years! Forty years! Margit! Good Lord! Too complicated! I drew away gently and started the car.—I am taking you home, Nicolette.—You'd make me very unhappy . . . —she sniffed. We didn't speak until we reached the hotel.—Until tomorrow—I said. But she didn't get out.—Until tomorrow—I said again. She shook her head violently.—Nicolette, don't you understand, it is impossible. Let me explain . . . She broke in angrily:—I understand everything, you fool, no need to explain. You want to tell me that you are deeply fond of Gaston, that you admire him, what he is to you, what you are to him, what he is to me. You think I don't know? What can you tell me that's new? Give me a cigarette! . . . I took out the pack, it was empty.—We'll do without one. Nicolette, listen to me . . . —I won't listen. You are going to talk rubbish. You are going to tell me what I already told myself. You want to tell me tonight what I told myself yesterday and the days before. Please, see again if you can find a cigarette! . . . I searched all my pockets but couldn't find one.

—Nicolette, let me . . . —Be quiet! You love me too! No use denying it!—Yes, but . . . —There is no but, don't you see? There is no but.—But there is. Friendship is sacred and . . . She snapped at me.—Is that all you see in me? Gaston's wife? Don't you understand that I am Nicolette? My body is not my mother's as she believed for a long time. My soul is not my father's as he believed for a long time.

My body and soul are mine, I dispose of them. It was I who gave them to Gaston. If I don't get a cigarette in a minute, I'll die . . .

I started the car. Slowly. I looked into every doorway. Nothing was open. In winter Firenze is dead, it doesn't effervesce as it does during the tourist season. I drove around the block. Everything was closed.—Do you have cigarettes in your room?—Yes.—Will you bring down two?—Yes . . . I drove to my hotel.—Can I come up with you?

—Nicolette, you know everything I was going to say, I admit it. But I felt Gaston and I were contemporaries. I can't push him back into the previous generation, as if he were my father. Or your grandfather. I can't turn him into an old cuckold . . . Nicolette looked at me with pity.—How naive can you get? He and I have an agreement. He doesn't mind. There's no cuckolding. Can I come up with you?

—Nicolette . . . if you . . . if you must . . . well, then pick a twenty-five year old . . . —Yes, sir, uncle, tomorrow I'll go to the market and buy myself a twenty-five year old. What's the price? Where do they sell them?—Nicolette, stop fooling. I am too old for you . . . Now she was laughing:—And so what? I, on the other hand, am too young for you. Thus, as you see, it evens out! (I didn't know what to say.)—All right. Can I come up?—No. I'll bring the cigarettes down.

I went up to my room and pocketed a pack of cigarettes. I returned to the car. It was empty. I ran to one corner, then the other, I searched the neighbourhood. She couldn't have gone very far. Finally, I gave up. She'll show up tomorrow. I went up to my room. As I put the key into the lock I had a thought. The Arno! She couldn't have . . . My heart was beating when I opened the door and put on the light. Nicolette was lying in my bed, smiling at me.

• 1 8 •

—Where were you all this time?
—I don't know. In many places.
—And you were not curious about me?
—I didn't even know you existed.
—It doesn't matter. Let's forget the past.
  Now you know. And only this is important.
—Now I know. And only this is important.

· 17 ·

Spring gurgles—
Spring gurgles, creek bubbles—
Spring gurgles, creek bubbles, brook rushes—
    Creek trickles—
    Creek trickles, brook rushes—
    Creek trickles, brook rushes, stream runs—
        Brook rushes—
        Brook rushes, stream runs—
        Brook rushes, stream runs, river flows—
            Estuary booms, pours, flows, churns, whirls, sobs—
                Ocean rocks—ocean rocks—ocean rocks—

·16·

—When did you decide that you would come up with me?

—During the concert.

—Why?

—I don't know. The music filled the hall and my head and my heart. And I thought only about you. And I could hardly wait for the concert to end. So that the music could begin.

—The music? I don't understand.

—Nor do I. You were the music.

—And yesterday?

—Yesterday I thought what a pity that it is impossible. That I am taboo. But today the music told me everything is possible. That there is no impossible. It flowed and it stormed. Like your poems.

—And if you hadn't gone to the concert today?

—The music was always there. But not outside. Today it was outside as well. And the two met. If I hadn't gone to the concert today... Then, something else would have happened tomorrow. For instance, a chocolate cake. And the inner sweetness would have replied to it. You are the sweetness. Just as you are the music. Something would have happened.

—You are terrible.

—Indeed?

—Not indeed. You are music and chocolate cake.

—You, too.

—I know. You, too.

—Me, too. I know. I know it too. Won't you come to bed?

—Not yet. Not yet. It still disturbs me.

—The age difference? Shall I go to the market?

—That doesn't disturb me anymore.

—Then what? Gaston?

—No. That doesn't disturb me, either.

—The horns?

—No, not that. He'll know. He can know about everyone but not about me. Nobody would bother him, but I would. It disturbs me that I have to lie. How will I look him in the eye? How will I feel afterwards? Or will I ever see him again?

—You won't lie to him. If you confessed, he would misunderstand. He would understand that we cheated him. Reality is a lie. At times you have to lie if you want to tell the truth.

—It sounds good. (Perhaps Mona Lisa will be the solution... I only thought this. I couldn't say it aloud.)

—Put out the light. And at last... light a cigarette, for me, too.

• 2 6 •

(I found this today on a bit of paper. I wrote it immediately after coming home. Broken sentences are all I found. I couldn't express myself. I wrote it one week before chapter 27. One week before the first chapter of this book.)

> I've moved into another time—
> It's noon here when it's night there—
> It's evening here when dawn breaks there—
> It's morning here when it's mid-afternoon there—
> You're in the middle distance of a single number
> (if I dial 0 on the telephone)

• 2 3 •

I wrote this on that last night when I could not see
        Nicolette any more.
In semi-sleep I recited the lines of a poem and I was dazed
        I couldn't stand on my feet,
Get up, switch on the light, look for paper and write the words
        so that they don't get lost,
I reassured myself, I shall not forget them, tomorrow morning
        I'll remember every word,
But next morning I left and since then all has changed around me,
        the landscape, time and faces,

I can no longer remember the words, I just write them down as they come,

        but this is no longer the same:

        "I shall return here one day . . ."
        (no, that's not it.)

        "He will return to the City
        when She is no longer there . . ."
        (almost)

        "He knew he would return one day
        to the City when she is no longer there
        and he knew the City would be cold . . ."
        (I can't do it!)

     I recited a poem to myself that night, in semi-sleep, about going back to Firenze one day, knowing what that day would be like: I shall roam the streets where I once walked with her and the warmth of my hand will be lonely—I shall sit in a car and the seat beside me will be empty—I shall look at the cascade of the Hotel Excelsior behind which a smile glitters, a voice rings today, and it will be mute and dark—maybe it will be summer but the City will be cold—the houses and squares will be brilliantly lit but I'll hear only the ululation of darkness—the towers and monuments will lift their heads but for me the street will be a crevice between dark houses—music will stream out of every café but I'll only hear a strangled scream . . .

     (Something like that but much more beautiful.)

· 2 5 ·

Firenze—New York—PanAmerican.

A single sentence clatters in my mind. A single sentence with small variations, the same sentence, the tone unchanged. During the whole flight, the same sentence:

—Back into the winter. Back into the night. Back into the cold. Back into the darkness. Back into the winter. Back into the night. Back into the cold winter. Back into the dark night. Back into the darkness.

(Back into the pre-Nicolette.)

(Into loneliness?)

(No.)

Back into death. Back into the underworld. Back into existence without Nicolette.

(Before Nicolette loneliness was negative.)

(After Nicolette loneliness is convex.)

(Before Nicolette loneliness was indifferent.)

(After Nicolette loneliness is a scream.)

Back into the winter, the snow, the ice, the night, the grey darkness, back into death.

(Nicolette!!!!!!!!!!!!!!!!!!!!!!!!!!)

• 4 8 •

I am unhappy.

Oh, how unhappy I am.

Oh, how unhappy I am. My suffering, lo, how great.

Hey! This doesn't sound bad at all.

Oh how unhap, Py I am. My sufferings. Lo how great.

My God! This is a poem!

Ohhowunhap, PyIam, Mysufferings, Lohowgreat.

Marvellous. Where's the pencil? Here. Paper? There.

Oh. How. Un. Hap. Py. I. Am.

Hallo? Joe? Nothing. Come up. Now? All right.

My. Suf. Fer. Ings. Lo. How. Great.

Hi, Joe. Sit down. I've written something. Will you listen?
Ohhowunhappylam. Mysufferingslohowgreat.
Truly? You like it? I think I didn't read it right. Wait again.
Ohhowun. Happyl. Am Mysuffer. Ingslohow. Great.
Do you think so? They'd publish it? I'll try!
Niterary Lews? May I bring it up? Thank you.
Yes this is the one. You'll publish it? How much? Only? All right.
Here it is. Page seventy-three. Nicely printed. Even illustrated. Hm.
Fifty thousand copies? Wonderful!
Oh, how unhappy I am . . . Beautiful!
Oh, how happy I am!

· 3 6 ·

—And here is my love—said Birabeau winking at me. Her name was Gerda, she was a Swiss girl. Perfect French, German, Italian. And English.

Birabeau loved one in every town. He had divorced his wife long ago. He was on a perpetual world-tour and had a girl-friend in every town.

—Robert, my friend. Hungarian.

Oh, Hungarian? I adore Hungarians. They are outspoken, honest, and they have some immoral morality that is hard to put into words. True?

—Yes. That of the oppressed. Because we've always been oppressed and what was immoral for the oppressor was moral for us. An internal morality. Revolutionary morality.

—That's it. The morality of survival.

Gerda is a nice girl. She reminds me of Nicolette. Around the nose and the mouth. Not the hair and not the voice. She is too slim. Well, who expects everything to be perfect? Birabeau rushes forth and back. From his dressing room to the stage, from the stage to the producer's office. From time to time he comes in and breaks into our conversation. He is nervous. We flit from one subject to the other, begin everything, finish nothing. Now she is telling me about her parents.

—Robert! Robert!

—Yes?

—Tomorrow Detroit. What shall I do last? The cantata or the trio?

I see Gerda once more for a moment. Exchange of telephone numbers and addresses.

—Robert!

—Yes?

—Forgive me but I forgot that you were coming today. I am invited to the Ambassador's but I cannot take you along. Angry?

—Not at all. My plane leaves in an hour.

—Then it's all right. You are not angry. How did you like Gerda?

—Nice. We could be friends.

—Nothing more?

—Nothing more. Besides, I am . . . you know. But she is also too thin. Not my cup of tea.

—Oh. But all right for a night, don't you think?

—I do. But not for me. For you.

—For me she'll be all right. I am not in love.

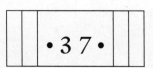

NEW TROOPS REVIEW

15. Before, in the car. (Too old, too young.) Nicolette offers herself.
16. Last clarification in my room.
(17.) First lovemaking. (Told in several languages.)
18. Afterwards. There are no pangs of conscience.
19. The evolution of "I love you."
20. I want to stay in the Now.
21. The same in Haiku.
22. The New Year's Eve reply.
23. Last night in Firenze without Nicolette.
24. The cut-off arm. (six experiments.)
25. In the aeroplane.
26. Broken words after arrival home.
27. First chapter written. Night and day Nicolette.
28. Same in Haiku (Experiments.)
29. Letter to Firenze. (Edith.)
30. 3 billion Anastasiuses.
31. Why I lied to Edith . . .
32.
33.
34.
35. Half-way along the novel's life.
36. Gerda.
37. This. (I'm approximately here in the writing.)
38.
39.
40.
41.
42.
43.
44.
45.
46.
47. The individual's aim.
48. The basic formula of artistic sublimation.
49. If I wrote a diary.
50. Transformation into poem. She and the Voice agree—against me.
∞. Unwritten. To be written. Freedom. Victory over Fate.

• 2 •

After my emigration from Hungary it took a few years before I could again write and direct films in Toronto. Then I could visit Gaston again in Paris. In almost all his paintings, an enchanting face looked down on me, followed me with its eyes, at times the central figure, at times a face in the crowd, a boy, a girl. I rubbed my temples . . . —Familiar?—asked Gaston, smiling.—I must have seen that face before . . . —I murmured.—Who is she?—My wife—said Gaston.—Oh. In that case I must be mistaken.—No, you aren't. You know her . . . I stared at him.—Nicolette—he replied, totally at ease.—That five year old . . . ?—She is eighteen now. Don't look so shocked. She's eighteen, yes. And I am fifty-eight. If your gaping means why did I marry her, the answer is simple. She married me. A year ago.

Little Nicolette...I had to sit down.—Is she at home?—Unfortunately, you came at the wrong time—said Gaston. She'll be in Paris only a month from now. She is on a trip around the world, I received her letter from Japan yesterday. But if you want a faint notion of who she is, look through these. (He placed an album in front of me.) It's a collection of newspaper articles. From the age of twelve to seventeen. They wrote more about her than about any statesman.

Gaston spent the afternoon painting. I read. About a hundred times during that afternoon, my imagination brought back little Nicolette standing up in her bed in her little pink nightshirt: "Where were you until now?" The same openness, the same un-compromising, bold sincerity, emerged in every article. Her adventures increased as the years went by but her character remained the same. The bare, curious spirit which refused to don conventional clothes on this earth. The unbending will which acquires what it wants at any price. At the age of twelve she was the child star of a film. The film played for years to full houses. She was offered a contract worth millions but refused it. By then she was bored with acting and was not interested in money. She took up ice skating and within a year became champion. At the age of fourteen she ran away with an expedition to Central Africa because her parents refused to let her go. She nursed natives who named a village after her. At fifteen, back in Paris, she was a beauty queen, wooed by a young millionaire, with villas in New Zealand, Florida, and Switzerland. In addition, he was Adonis. All the girls envied Nicolette, but she rejected him. "Only" because she was not in love with him. The millionaire killed himself, but Nicolette was already engaged in a women's chess championship. Random examples of what Nicolette was doing every month, every week, always.

Gaston looked up when I put the album on the table.—
Well?... I remained silent for some moments. Everything I'd read
was whirling in my head. What I finally said sounded something like
this:—Well... this little, beautiful, amiable wife of yours has had
more lives than some old men... Gaston broke into laughter:—You
see, there's no generation gap between us! You'd hardly think of her
as a teenager, would you? But the hard fact is that she still is!—A
unique phenomenon—I said. Someone who always knows what she
wants. And she always gets it. She is always sincere. And always
uninhibited. Straightforward, swift, irresistible. If an arrow could
have a soul... if everything the papers say about her is true.

—It is all true. What the papers say is "nothing but the truth" as
they say in court. But Nicolette is much more than that. "The whole
truth" is known perhaps only to me.

—My impression is that Nicolette begins all sorts of things, gets
tired of them very quickly, and is, so to say, fickle. She yields to stray
impulses which soon burn themselves out.

Gaston nodded.—I knew this is what you'd think. But that's
only how it appears on the surface: she never left anything un-
finished. Her capriciousness is only a semblance. The truth
is... I've never tried to put it into words... I am not a writer...

—You mean that behind all the bits and pieces there is a
cohesive force? Some sort of system serving a definite purpose?

Gaston's eyes looked into the distance.—A system? No. The
word is far too pedestrian. Nicolette... Nicolette is a messenger.
Here on a mission.

—Where? In France?

—No. On Earth.

—...

—Next time you come I may be able to make you understand,
in my language. Not in words. In six months... or a year... I am
working on it now.

• 3 •

A year later, when I returned to Paris, Nicolette was away. Gaston took my arm:—Now, don't be annoyed. Perhaps it's better that she shouldn't be here. You may get to know her better.

He took me to the second floor of his house. It had been a loft. He had turned it into his second studio. The room was in utter darkness. He switched on the light. The wall was covered with a single, gigantic painting. It hit me like a thunderbolt.

Fractional happenings were here united into an organic whole. It seemed to me that the painting was in movement. I couldn't utter a word. The painting was timeless: Leonardo, Michelangelo, Giotto, Hokusai, El Greco had painted it with Gaston's hand, within its frame the cultures of India, China, Africa, America merged, it could have been the work of a French painter or an Italian, of a primitive, a romantic or an impressionist, Egyptian picture writing or the art of photography. Still, it was one work, the work of one painter, and looking at it one felt that it had always existed, that it had only to be discovered.

—New mythology...—I whispered, and Gaston replied quietly:—Or only a character study. If you prefer: a portrait.

It was only then that I understood Nicolette's mission and the painting followed me, until its crystal clear lucidity, transcendent, its ancient roots in ourselves, its modern presence irritated me, disturbed me, inspired me...

Finally one evening I was compelled to translate it into a poem.

• 4 •

And it happened that Zeus-Jupiter,
Father of the gods, flung lightning
From angry eyes, his voice shaking Olympus:
"Into my presence, I order the fugitive:
At once, bring the saucy muse, Nicolette,
Who, when I approached, driven by divine desire,
Escaped from my embrace to mix with terran worms,
And now inspires that paltry mud-bound lot
to words of flame, dance and soaring music,
She leaves me trembling, unquenched in my desire . . ."
While yet his voice echoed round the chambers

Up rose Cyclops from the shadowed Earth
And led forth Nicolette, proud though in chains.
Uncontained, the anger of the God flamed forth:
"Fugitive, you who cunningly escaped,
Now must you humbly repent your sin,
Tremble with fear at my well-deserved ire!"
"Were you to speak more softly"—came the reply
From Nicolette—"Perhaps we could agree.
Understand, I will not beg for mercy.
From the fire-filled earth this one-eyed slave
Dragged me here. Nor do I acknowledge a sin.
Your anger frightens me not."
Wide gaped the eyes of Jupiter in disbelief:
"Hah, you insignificant tenth muse,
Blot on the glory of my invincible army
Dare you speak flippantly to the god of gods?
Who are you? And where lies your strength
If my strength ceases to bolster yours?"
"I am I,"—replied Nicolette—
"And singleness of purpose resists all violence
If my desire responds, I can be yours,
If not, I shall nick the edge of your lightning,
Mute the storms of your cerebral passion,
And tumble from its base, your game,
The solitary creation of the world.
Thus, wait your turn, dare not humiliate me,
For the snakes of lies and hypocrisy
Nest elsewhere, not in my breast.
Punish me if you will, but your self-indulgence
Cannot enslave me. If I want you,
Dream not of escape. But if I don't,
Forget at once your own desire."

"Perish then," screamed Zeus, "you grain of sand
Who dare defy the Most Powerful!" And
Hefting his sword of flame Nicolette he hacked
In pieces, then blew into his hundred-fluted
Trumpet, and Nicolette's dust rose and scattered
Through space. And where it fell Nothing emerged
As Something, a little space of light and being
Alitheia—a universe birthing.
If the dust landed on a tree, the tree
Burst into bud, then into blood-red blossom.
When breathed by those of earth the particles
Flowered into word, paint, music and design,
A world of spirit working to disarm
The fateful sword of violence divine.

And in this way, Nicolette's unconquered will
Roamed the earth, a thousand shapes of women,
Whose hearts of love brought down Olympus
On the heads of its tyrannical gods.

• 3 2 •

My love,

Firenze is still here and in it am I. Still, nothing is as it was when you
were here as well. I walk our streets and they are empty. Yet many
people walk in them. I sit in our café and it is silent. Yet, it is noisy.
Yesterday, I passed our nightclub. Its door was like a yawn. My days
are nights without you. You are with me only in my dreams. Often I
wake and reach out for you. It is dreadful to wake to the realization
that your place beside me is empty. At such times even the moon is
not what it was. Do you remember the walnut tree in the garden?
Long ago—even five days may have gone by since then—we and it

were conspirators. Now, it is but an old beggar nodding against the window. I couldn't even say good-bye to you, my love. I couldn't even give you a last kiss. I couldn't even see you. When we parted on the 30th of December we didn't even know this was our last meeting. We were supposed to see each other the next day. But then Gaston's friends arrived and I had to spend New Year's Eve with them. It was torment. And that last telephone conversation... inventing code-words so that they wouldn't understand us, pretending to be cool so that they wouldn't notice our love . . . it drove me mad that we were so near and still I couldn't see you. You had to return home on the first day of the year. And I immediately moved into your hotel, into your room, on the main floor. I don't know if that was wise. It is bad, because it reminds me of you and you are far away. But it is also good because it reminds me of you although you are far away. But good or bad, I had to do it. I could not stay in my old place because I am no longer the old me. You changed me into someone else. My smile is different, my eye flashes differently, my movements are new. I should like to stand on the hill next to David and shout my happiness to the world. And my unhappiness. Why does one have to lose happiness right after finding it? I am afraid to return to Gaston. Perhaps I shall tell him everything. But I cannot do that because of you. Perhaps, I shall reply mysteriously: "Yes, I met Robert, but don't ask me anything. You were never interested, don't be now." Perhaps, I shall lie, for the first time in my life. But then, I am so happy and I should like Gaston to know it too. I am completely confused. It is also possible that my role in Gaston's life has come to an end. For the first time in five years he is using another model. Perhaps I'll ask for a divorce when I get home. I don't know anything, with one exception. I want you. When you have finished your work, try and come back. If it isn't possible, come to Paris as soon as you can. And if everything remains unchanged and I am still with Gaston, pretend that you are after Véronique. Use her in order to keep me a secret. Dishonest? Believe me, it is not. If I lie, it won't be for myself. It will be for Gaston to save him suffering. And for you and for the friendship between the two of you. I wish he'd divorce me! We'll see . . . Come back, my love, if you can. Firenze is still here and in it am I. Firenze waits for you and I wait with it. Let us resuscitate this dead town together. Come back. Fly back.

Nicolette

· 3 3 ·

My love,

I received your letter. The same day you wrote it I also wrote something. The 27th chapter of an unwritten, and perhaps never-to-be-written, novel. The same thoughts, the same words. The two halves of the divided YouandI throb to the same rhythm. I am homesick for Firenze here, you there. One doesn't have to leave to be homesick. You hurt, like a cut-off arm continues to hurt the soldier. You are not here but I always feel you near me and I talk to you. I'll try to finish my work as quickly as possible and fly back to your arms, your body. But if I can't make it, we'll meet in Paris. Don't be hasty, don't do anything silly. Gaston mustn't know about me whatever happens. Don't hurt him. I'll find someone to help me keep you secret. Not Véronique, I don't want to "use" her, she doesn't deserve it. Someone else. This letter has to remain short because today I am off to New York to see Birabeau. If only I could write the letter I am writing to you every minute of the day . . .

Robert

• 5 •

Only last year did I meet Nicolette personally. I was in Paris for a short time only and there was no hotel room to be had for two weeks. For a day or two, yes. I was not in the mood, nor did I have the time, to move six times in two weeks.—Don't be an idiot, there's plenty of room here, you'll be in nobody's way—said Gaston. I accepted his invitation.

I spent my days running around, talking with editors, translators, film directors and actors. And in the evenings I went with Véronique to the theatre, to the cinema. She is a young poet, a communist and very talented. Her words are like dark rocks, expressing her beautiful dreams of the future constructed of straight iron beams. We walked hand in hand, roamed the dark Paris streets kissing, and I spent more nights in her tiny room under the eaves than in Gaston's house.—Oh, you are the one who stole my friend from me!—said Gaston when I introduced him to Véronique.—And he's the man who worried about finding a room to stay!...

Nicolette arrived unexpectedly, like a tornado. The three of us were having dinner together when she showed up. She'd just arrived from abroad. She kissed Gaston.—Is there any food left for me? I am starving... Then, she turned to me:—Oh, you are Robert, aren't you? I recognized you from your picture in the papers. At last we meet... We love your poems.—Thank you—I replied.—There is one I wrote about you before we even met.—Indeed? You'll show it to us soon, won't you? she said lightly, like someone who is used to having poems written about her. She turned to Véronique and greeted her. It took them less than a second to know and dislike each other. Yet both of them were rebels. Véronique professionally and collectively. Nicolette in her blood, in her entire life.

During dinner Gaston mentioned jokingly that this was our second meeting, the first took place seventeen years before.—Then it is not surprising that I shouldn't remember it—laughed Nicolette.

This is how we met the first time. After that we ran into each other several times in the house, in the kitchen, in the street. We liked each other. But we didn't see each other. For me, she was Gaston's wife. To her, I was Gaston's friend.

· 3 4 ·

Cher Robert,

When are you coming again? I miss you. I've written three letters already but I tore them up. Perhaps it will surprise you that I suddenly emerge from the long forgotten *"neige d'antan."* God knows how many loves you've had since then, perhaps you have completely forgotten me. When are you coming again? I miss you. I spent three months in prison because of an anti-government poem. It was a good poem. Still, I don't know if it was worth it. I've thought a lot about your fantastic theories. Perhaps you are right when you say that building my own individual life, I would build a future just as much as with this artificial zealousness. "The future grows anyway like an embryo, pre-programmed." When are you coming again? I miss you. The movement hasn't changed, the comrades are loyal, reliable, but boring. Somehow, all my friends have scattered. I go to other cafés, not there. When are you coming again? I miss you. You could have written at least one letter. Have you thought about us at all during this past year? I have. Write, if you have the time. And come again. I miss you.

Véronique

· 39 ·

Each love affair ends
when you begin to suffer
in the next.

• 3 8 •

How I yearned for Véronique a year ago! And how many poems I wrote about her without sending them off. She doesn't know about it even today, she never received a letter from me. Perhaps it is for the best. She'd wait for me even more impatiently. Her every second sentence recalls me to Paris. And I am going. I am flying as soon as I can. But it is not Véronique I shall see.

· 3 9 ·

Your love is dead
only when the next love
begins to ache.

• 16 •

I shall try again to approach the conversation we had before
Nicolette became mine . . . before I became hers . . . before we became each other's . . . and before we created the YouandI. But now I
hold a magnifying glass in my hand and with it I magnify the individual details. As in the films, where the "long shot" gives your eye
the overall scene, then the lens shifts to "close up" to get a detail.

> I placed the key into the lock . . . The Arno!
> Perhaps Nicolette . . . ! It cannot be. But I of-
> fended her. Her female vanity. Life is so cheap
> for the young, nowadays . . . Judy, Jean-Paul,

how many I knew...A little wound on the ego, a sudden change of mood and they throw away life as if it were a worn-out shirt... Nicolette offered herself. I rejected her. She jumped. The filthy, stagnant river. Deep. She holds her nose. Something bursts. She is sinking...I open the door. The room is dark. I should go back. This thought! Perhaps she didn't. Where's the light switch...But perhaps she did. Perhaps she is just about to, and I'd get there in time. I feel faint. A second and I'll collapse. I must regain my strength. I turn around. Good Lord! Who is that? There she was all the time, waiting for me in my bed. She smiles.—Thank God...thank God!... I fall to my knees beside the bed and bury my head in her two hands.

Another close-up:

—Unfaithful. Stupid word. Nobody can be unfaithful to anybody. It's only yourself you can be unfaithful to. What is marriage? An institution. What does it institutionalize? Love. What is love? A delusion. Accumulated sexual energy. Nothing else. Marriage is an accumulation of unfaithfulness. The institutionalization of a delusion. But time rots away the institution, and it unmasks the delusion. The sexual energy accumulates anew until it finds a new object. The new passion may last so long that the lovers would die before it ends. It is still temporary, sooner or later it must collapse. Shall we prop up that mouldy institution with planks? Shall we idolize the mask of delusion instead of the real faces behind it? It is better if we demolish the ruin and be unfaithful to unfaithfulness.

Another close-up:

—I adore Gaston like a God. I love you as a man. Why I married him? Because he needed me. Because it was me he needed in order to become a God. Because, when I married him, he was only a divine man. But now my mission is accomplished. He no longer needs me. Perhaps he doesn't know it yet but I do.

The last close-up:

—While you do what others expect from you, you are a slave. But you cannot live miserably cowed. Love is freedom. Most people gabble about freedom, many whine for it, others adore it as a cloud-bodied god. And yet, it is all so simple. All you have to do is dare straighten up. You just need courage to be free. If I tell you to be brave, I tell you to be free. And if I tell you to be free, I tell you: Love me!

$\cdot$ 17 $\cdot$

—You don't mind, now, if I kiss you?
—I'd mind, now, if you didn't kiss me.
—Then I'll kiss you now.
—Kiss mmm . . .

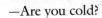

—Are you cold?
—A little.
—Shall I close the window?
—Yes, do. But don't draw the curtains. It's a full moon.
—Is this all right?
—Yes.

—Turn out the light.

—Where are you going?

—My shoes bother me. My dress bothers me. My bra
bothers me.

—I forgot how you look. Let me see. That's your face.
Your ear. Your nose. Your neck. Your ear. Your bottom. Your belly. Your thigh. Your knee.

—Now you know?

—Yes. I am blind. I saw you with my fingers.

—Can you see with your mouth as well?

—Don't worry.

—How warm your hand is!

—And how cold your bottom is!

—Take off your clothes, you, too.

—Do you like this?

—It's wonderful. Oh . . .

—Don't bite.

—It's easy to say. I feel like devouring you.

—Won't you miss me then?

—I love you!

—Be gentle. Don't get so fierce.

—Like this . . . ?

—Yes . . . yes . . . this is good . . . so good . . . oh

—And now let's smoke a cigarette.

—All right. Put on the light.

—Here you are.

—Thank you. Oh, my eyes . . .

—I can't see either.

—Your face is all smoothed out.

—You too are more beautiful.

—I can feel it. You made me beautiful.

—You smoothed out my face.

—You are welcome.

—Thank you.

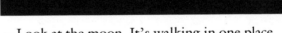

—Look at the moon. It's walking in one place.

—It isn't good like this. Shall I put out the light?

—Yes, do. We can talk in the dark as well.

—But I cannot see you.

—And what about your mouth?

—Like this?

—Oh . . . I've never . . . felt like this . . . oh

—Cigarette?

—The light?

—All right?

—All right.

—Listen!

—Yes?

—I've discovered something strange.

—Tell me.

—Gaston is gone.

—What?

—My conscience doesn't bother me. I thought it would, terrible. I feel nothing.

—That's wonderful . . .

—I don't feel that I've cheated Gaston. I don't feel you are his wife. You are Nicolette. My Nicolette.

—That's what I am.

—Sweetheart, darling.

—My darling love.

—Do you love me?

—You know it. Don't ask.

—But say it. I want to hear it.

—I love you. I love you. I love you. Do you love me?

—No.

—No?

—I adore you.

—Then put out the light.

—Look at the moon.

—The moon looks at us.

—At us?

—At us.

—What's this?

—A pimple.

—I'll kiss it.

—You are mad.

—Let me. It's yours.

—That's not the pimple anymore, you crook...oh...
ah...

—I'll kiss you now from top to toe. I'll start with your
neck and finish with your feet.

—Have you a return ticket?

—I have. But not all the way. Only to...

—What are you looking at?

—You.

—Since when have you been looking at me?

—A minute only. I just woke up.

—You too?

—Me too. Almost simultaneously.

—Everything happens simultaneously, doesn't it?

—Everything. With us, everything.

—It's morning.

—Are you hungry?

—Yes. And you?

—You don't have to ask, you should know. If you are hungry, I am hungry too. Everything is simultaneous.

—Of course. Look.

—At what?

—It isn't there.

—What isn't there?

—The moon.

—Right. The moon isn't there.

—Let there be Light!

—. . . and there was light.

—And the light was bright.

—. . . unlike the night.

—Beside me, you turned into a poet overnight!

—True. Morning is so un-poetic. It's daybreak.

—I wish it were break-fast.

—There will be break-fast!

—Let there be break-fast!

—Fantastic idea. You eat. I eat. Simultaneously. The YouandI will eat break-fast. Wow!

—So? Do we get up?

—What? No good-bye?
—Yes. Good-bye . . . you . . .
—Is that going to be a good-bye kiss?
—No. It is going to be a see-you-again kiss.
—Then it's all right.

· 18 ·

—I feel marvellous.
—So do I.
—I don't mean physically.
—Nor do I.
—Psychologically.
—Me too.
—Of course, physically too.
—Of course, me too.
—But I've no conscience pangs. Gaston's face was there only until you became mine. Then it disappeared.
—That's wonderful.

—Until now you were taboo. Now you are you. You are you. Do
you understand?
—You, too, became you to me only now. Until now I didn't see
you.
—Did you begin to see me suddenly?
—No. Gradually.
—How?

That we met when I was five years old, in bed,
I don't remember, of course.

—First, Gaston mentioned it a year ago. At that dinner, in
Paris. When you were with Véronique. That was the first time
when I really met you. I'd heard a lot about you. You were like
an old friend. Immediately. But I didn't see you.

—When you showed up at my hotel in Firenze two weeks ago,
I was delighted to see you. You were clever, witty, sparkling,
nice. And you told me about Gaston. How the two of you be-

came friends. And you also told me about me. About what I told you in bed.

—Where were you until now?
—In many places.
—You weren't curious about me?
—I didn't even know you existed.
—It doesn't matter. But don't forget it in the future.
—You think I'd be able to forget it?

—It felt good to be with you. But I didn't see you. And I had to go to Venice. I was interested in Maurizio.

—I didn't see you even when you came to Venice. We were to-gether for about three hours. I was depressed. Maurizio had been a disappointment. He is no real artist. Nothing but a bohemian. Nor is he a real man. Only a bohemian. He treated me badly. He'll never amount to anything. He'll disappear. He doesn't need me.

—When you came to Firenze again I'd gotten over Maurizio. But I still didn't see you. After Maurizio I didn't feel like a woman. You were a friend. Every day closer.

—One evening you spoke about yourself. You told me your life. Then, I felt very close to you. You spoke about your loves. I felt that it was good to be with you. Good and comfortable. And interesting. And exciting. I always knew you were gifted. But it's one thing to read a book and another to hear yourself in the flesh.

—Then it was my turn. I told you everything there was to tell about myself. All the boys. The first. Before Gaston and during Gaston. I already felt that I owed you this. To show you that I, too, had imagination, not only you. I complained to you about Maurizio. Then, you uttered a sentence which rang on in my mind. "If you weren't taboo to me, I'd be the best solution for you just now."

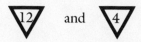

and

—The next evening I went up to your room. We were already friends. Very close friends. And already I saw you. You spoke about your plans, your marriage. I became a part of you. About Gaston, about art. About the effect of his paintings on your poetry. And then you read me the poem you had written about me when you didn't even know me yet. And I remembered that it had happened to me. That what you had written had indeed happened to me, I remembered it although it never had happened. I felt that you wanted to kiss me. And I, too, wanted to kiss you. But it wasn't the proper place. And it wasn't the proper time. I almost fled. After that Homeric hymn it would simply not have been in style.

—The next day you asked me what I wanted to do: go with you to the Club or go with a young journalist to a concert. I wanted to be with you but I was still struggling against it, so I chose the concert. The music filled the hall and my soul. Yet, I could hardly wait for it to be over and for you to come for me. As if that young journalist hadn't been there at all. Music had enlightened me. It blew away the taboo. You know the rest. But if I look back now I feel that it had always been you whom I loved. And sooner or later I should have discovered it. And sooner or later I would have seduced you as I seduced you last night.

$$\boxed{\cdot\,1\;8\,\cdot}$$

—Let me tell you the Secret, Nicolette. You did not seduce me. I seduced you. But cunningly, craftily, imperceptibly . . .

—When I first saw you in bed, at the age of five, I immediately fell in love with you. This, of course, sounds ludicrous. But it was somewhere inside me that you would be my true woman if you were twenty years older.

—I had the same feeling when Gaston showed me his album about you. I didn't tell him. I didn't even admit it to myself.

—When I saw the painting, it told me something entirely different from what Gaston had tried to say in it. He painted that Zeus had given you to him. And I felt that Gaston-Zeus will give you to me. That is when it became conscious.

—When I saw you for the first time (for the second time), I was with Véronique. So there was a kind of honour. And Gaston. Unconsciously I compared you with Véronique and I wouldn't have minded a switch. If. If there hadn't been ifs.

—I didn't know for sure that I'd be coming to Firenze as well. I had business in Rome, in Milan, in Venice. Not in Firenze. I wanted to come and I didn't. Only to see Firenze again. But when I received Gaston's letter, I knew that I would come.

Not with the purpose of making you my own. All I wanted was to see you. You attracted me like a magnet. I had to come.

—I went straight to your hotel. But you were just on your way to Venice.

—When I passed through Venice there were a thousand things I should have done. But I spent the entire afternoon with you and put off my business until the following week.

—You always escaped me. Twice in Paris and here, too. You escaped me. I went back to Firenze to catch you at last. I didn't lie to you. I really idolize Gaston. I. But only one of my selves. The other courted you, calculatingly. The third watched the other two and laughed. The fourth was enraged at the one who watched. And while one of my selves was filled with the sanctity of friendship, the other told you devious stories about me, first to make you like me, then to make you desire me. When you "offered yourself" to me in the car, one of my selves congratulated itself that the fruit was ripe, ready for the plucking, but my third self clapped a hand on its mouth, allowing my second self to stutter, afraid to look upon the sacred taboo. In the meantime, my honest self went to bed and slept because somehow it was pushed back to the fifteenth place, and the fourth kept watching and taking notes. Then, my first self freed itself from the stronghold of the third and, imitating the bleating of the second, fed the fire of your desire by pretending innocence, as Joseph did once with Potiphar's wife. You seduced me but I tempted you, Nicolette, to seduce me. It was all my work, Nicolette. I am an old fox, an old diplomat of love . . .

• 1 4 •

What inanities you utter, you, Nicolette and Robert,
in rambling chapters,
puppets on a ramshackle puppet-stage,
seeking excuses in self-defence, blaming
each other and yourselves, unravelling
your cotton-wool insides, analysing each
strand separately, but you do not and cannot
look backward; an invisible string knots itself
around your skin, woven of cheap cotton,
a string knotted to my fingers,
so that you gambol ludicrously, your arms and legs

flapping and flopping when you talk, walk,
make love, eat and drink, purse your lips,
revolve your eyes stupidly as I pull the string,
imitate your male-deep, your woman-thin
voices: for years I've pulled you
toward each other, weaving the conspiratorial threads
I throw you against each other, fling you
upon each other in bed, my puppets, and
I talk about myself in your voices
when you speak of the YouandI, because I enjoy this
tiny Lilliputian comedy . . .
go on believing your entanglement created me,
I don't mind, let it be, let it be,
but tomorrow I'll tie another puppet to my right finger,
a new partner for Nicolette,
or perhaps another puppet on my left, to give Robert
a little variety, and I'll lend thousands of names to
thousands of puppets in the years to come,
but always I will stand behind them, I: "YouandI."

$\boxed{\cdot\ 18\ \cdot}$

—And now, which of your many selves loves me?
—All of them.

·40·

Sunday morning. The telephone rings.—Gerda... At first, I don't even know who Gerda is.—Birabeau's friend from New York. (Oh, the girl who resembles Nicolette!)—Let's meet this afternoon.

I take her to a café. She is wearing a skirt. She isn't as skinny as she seemed in her maxi. Shapely. A sweet little face.

Problems. She's been with a boyfriend for a year now. A nice boy, limited intelligence. A politician. Then Birabeau showed up, picked her out among the girls working at the academy of music. For one night only. She's the one in her town. There is but one Birabeau. After Birabeau, the boy was disappointing. They were constantly quarrelling. When she was young, her spirit had soared.

The politician's spirit, his ideas, were pedestrian. Now, Birabeau was living proof that she'd been right about herself.

—And why did you come to Toronto?

—Several reasons. To rest. I've had an awful week. Got to get away from it all. I have to work next week again. Also, to meet you. Lord, I'll die if you don't give me a cigarette!

—Here. Why'd you want to meet me?

—Several reasons. To ask you for help. Advice. And because I felt we'd be good friends. And because last time we couldn't talk. Everything was fragmented. And...

—And?

—...and I don't know.

I park my car in front of the house where she stays. I tell her about Nicolette.—...and you remind me of her. She hurts. You are here. May I kiss you?...She lets me. One kiss. More kisses. Wild kissing.—You have a nice mouth.—So have you.—I am not in love with you,—I tell her frankly—but you're a wonderful escape from my problems.—I know. You are the same for me.—I am only using you.—I know. I am using you, too.—Will you invite me for a cup of coffee?—No. Not today. It's not the proper place, nor the proper time. I'm confused even without you. Perhaps next time. Come to New York.

• 40 • and • 15 • and • 12 •

"It isn't proper place. It isn't proper time."—said Gerda yesterday as did Nicolette a month ago.

Even when asking for a cigarette she used the same words, expressed the same greed.

Apropos. I have looked through what I've written so far. I always wanted to tell and always forgot, the brand we smoked that night when, from the depths of the Arno, she materialized in my bed.

Nationali.

I still cherish that packet.

• 4 1 •

This is unbearable. Always Nicolette, Nicolette, Nicolette. I am beginning to bore myself. It seems that maybe in February I can return to Firenze. Probably. But if not, then to Paris in March. This is certain.

I suffer. I search the face of every woman for her beauty. I can't find it.

Esmeralda, the Jamaican typist, wants to come up to my place during lunch break. I put it off again and again. What for? Nothing would happen between us. Nicolette would paralyze me.

One evening I took Lisa home in my car. She didn't get out for a long time. Her lips shone in the dusk.—When do we meet again?—I asked after a while.—It depends only on you...—she replied.

Juliette telephoned. She is going to the theatre but will be home at midnight. Do I feel like coming up?

Lorna gave me her telephone number. She'd like to talk with me about "literature." Every time we meet in the corridor she blushes.

And I pass up every opportunity. When I've nothing to do, I write this.

Also, when I'm busy, I write this. I neglect everything else. Ten times a day—ten times ten every day—I recall our first night.

17.

17.   17.

                    17.   17.

        17.   17.   17.   17.

    17.   17.   17.

        17.   17.   17.

            17.   17.   17.

17.   17.

17.   17.   17.

    17.   17.

                17.   17.

    17.   17.

17.   17.   17. 17.   17.

17.   17.

        17.   ⟨ 1 7 ⟩   17.

    17.   17.   17.

17.   17.   17.

        17.   17.   17.

17.   17.   17.

            17.   17.   17.

17.   17.

        17.   17.   17.

                17.   17.

        17.   17.   17.

17.   17.   17.

            17.   17.   17.

17.   17.

17.   17. 17.   17.

                    17.   17.

17.   17.   17.

    17.   17.

            17.   17.

• 4 3 •

I write this book at night.
I sleep until noon every single day.
Every afternoon I type what I wrote the night before.
Every single night I write this book.
I am obsessed.
Nicolette no longer matters.
Only "Nicolette" is important.
I don't miss Nicolette.
I only miss the missing part of "Nicolette."
The missing part I must write.
I don't think about Nicolette anymore. (Ohhow. Happy. Iam.)

"Nicolette" is not Nicolette.

More starry-eyed. Slimmer.

After "Nicolette," Nicolette is disappointing.

Nicolette is nearly like my wife.

"Nicolette" is my child.

She's more important. Nicolette and I will die.

"Nicolette" may survive us.

Do I love Nicolette? I don't know.

Am I in love with "Nicolette"? That's for sure.

Do I want to meet Nicolette?

I don't know.

I'd love to meet "Nicolette." In real life.

I wonder where she is?

•44•
FINAL SURVEY

−1. FATE

0. FOREWORD

1. PARIS STUDY TRIP, FIRST MEETING WITH NICOLETTE. Robert recalls it while reading the album (2). Gaston recalls it at the Paris dinner (5). Robert tells Nicolette about it (7). They both recall it (18).

2. PARIS VISIT YEARS LATER, THE ALBUM. Robert tells Nicolette about it (18).

3. GASTON'S PAINTING. Robert tells Nicolette about it (18).

4. POEM ABOUT THE TENTH MUSE. Robert mentions it to Nicolette (5). Robert reads it to Nicolette (12). Nicolette tells Robert about it (18).

5. SECOND FIRST MEETING WITH NICOLETTE IN PARIS. VÉRONIQUE. Nicolette's version (18). Robert's version (18).

6. GASTON'S LETTER. Robert tells Nicolette about it (18).

7. FIRST MEETING IN FIRENZE. Nicolette's version (18). Robert's version (18).

8. MEETING IN VENICE. Nicolette's version (18) Robert's version (18).

9. SECOND MEETING IN FIRENZE. Nicolette's version (18). Robert's version (18).

10. GETTING CLOSE IN FIRENZE. Nicolette's version (18). Robert's version (18).

11. FIRENZE, THAT SENTENCE (If you weren't taboo to me . . ."). Nicolette's version (18). Robert's version (18).

12. IN FIRENZE NICOLETTE LISTENS TO A POEM ABOUT HERSELF (4). Nicolette's version (18). Robert's version (18). Robert is reminded of it by Gerda (40&15&12).

13. FIRENZE, THE CONCERT. Nicolette's version (18). Robert's version (18).

14. YOUANDI'S MONOLOGUE WHEN NICOLETTE AND ROBERT DO NOT HEAR IT. Fragments of it will reach Robert's subconscious later on (20).

15. BEFORE IT, IN THE CAR. NICOLETTE OFFERS HERSELF. Old & young (15). The whole conversation (15). Robert is reminded of it by Gerda (40&15&12).

16. BEFORE IT, IN THE HOTEL ROOM. Close-ups (16).

17. THE FIRST LOVE MAKING. Its rhythm (17). Its chronology (17). Its mood (17). Its lyrics (17). Its memory (17).

18. AFTERWARDS. No pangs of conscience (18). "Where were you all this time?" (18).

My God, I never thought of it before! . . . If this book is ever published, Gaston will know everything!

· 4 5 ·

It's done. This is the last page. But it won't go at the end, of course. After all, a book must be edited. Even if it's supposed to look unedited. The last page should repeat the first. This is the internal pattern I project into all my works. The circle is closing. But not completely. It continues over itself like a spiral. The end is the beginning and its opposite. It begins with fate and ends with freedom. It begins spontaneously and ends in an edited form. The chapter first written (27) was an independent short story from an unwritten and not-to-be-written novel. The last chapter (27) closes the written novel. Two weeks ago I didn't know that a novel was being written by me. Incredible! I have to put this page before the trip to Firenze.

I have to renumber Gaston's letter from 5 to 6 because I didn't count the Homeric poem. Two chapters, 42 and 44, are missing. I miscalculated a bit. Not to worry. I have been writing until eight in the morning and I am tired. I beg the reader to take out numbers 49 and 50, so that 48 will be the last chapter before the sign of the Infinite. And, on the right, let him push up the titles by two. Or . . . I've got a better idea. I'll write another survey and that will be chapter 44. I'll put it in front of this so the reader can see what I am talking about. Then only one chapter will be missing. And that one I'll write. What's that for me? Which one is it? 42. Well, what'll I write? Something beautiful, divine . . .

• 4 2 •

The bud which springs into flower on the stem.
Or the act of love.
Or the creation of the world.
Or this novel.
They are all the same.
I met Nicolette one month ago.
She inspired "Nicolette."
"Nicolette" is bigger than Nicolette.
"Nicolette" brought on the bud, the sexual organ, God,
    and all that remains to create.
I, too, became more by it.

From a dry branch, a branch bearing buds.

From a lonely man, a loving-lovemaking man.

From the scribbler of scattered poems, the author of a complete novel.

God.

Who created a world in six days.

And now I am tired.

And I say: Let there be a Seventh Day.

And there was.

—   —   —

—   —

–   .

. .

.

January 25, 1972

• 4 6 •

I've booked my flight to Firenze. I am leaving tomorrow morning. Firenze is still there and waiting for me. Nicolette is still there waiting for me. The thick frontier will disappear. I shall be happy.

Is Firenze really waiting for me? I'm sure everything will be different. I'm sure Nicolette will be different. It's possible she's in love with someone else. Perhaps my coming will be a painful surprise. Perhaps I won't love her anymore. Can one bring back the past? Perhaps I'll regret not having kept that beautiful memory exactly as it was.

But perhaps everything will be as it was in December. As if I'd never left. Although . . .

Gerda is sweet. And I want her. Perhaps I should go to New York instead. That Gerda even hurts a tiny bit. And how was that line? Every love ends when the next one begins to hurt.

If I waited one more month, perhaps I'd pine for Gerda and Nicolette would be like Véronique now.

Which would be practical, because then I could go and see Véronique in Paris.

What's more, I could see Nicolette as well. Why not? Everyone. So no one and nothing would hurt, ever.

Rubbish. I've been thinking of Nicolette for weeks and now that I have my ticket, I am not even happy.

I want to be happy. Nicolette is waiting for me. But I don't even miss Nicolette, because I've written "Nicolette." So, why am I going?

Gaston had thrown down Nicolette for me from Olympus and Nicolette has fulfilled her mission with me as well. Our child's name is "Nicolette." A manuscript, 150 pages long.

I'll show it to her some day. She may enjoy it. Perhaps she won't even understand it. Perhaps she will understand it, but will not like it. Does it matter? I like it, and only that is important.

The best thing would be to return the ticket. It's a lot of money. I'd rather buy a . . .

Now my heart jumps. Her arm. Her smile. Her eye. Her heat. Her kiss. Nicolette. I'm sure she still loves me. I'm sure everything will be as it was before. As if I'd never left.

• ∞ •

A little dark man sits across from me in the aeroplane.
  —I want to live.
  —Forget it.
  —I want to write.
  —Forget it.
  —I want to be happy.
  —Forget it.
  —I want Nicolette. I want the now. The eternal now.
  —Forget it.
  What a pest he is with his pentagonal head. I can read his lips. I
pick him up, lift him, fling him out through the closed window.

He gesticulates ridiculously in the air. He shouts: "I am Fate!" He grows smaller and sinks into the ocean.

I sit up straight. I am happy. I am free. I am brave. I am in love. My conscience bothers me not at all.

• 2 7 •

I'll arrive in the middle of the night. I'll take a taxi to the *pensione*. The garden gate will open. I'll slink soundlessly through the garden to the old walnut tree. I'll climb in through the half-open window and step out of my clothes. My place will be there to the left of Nicolette. Lightly, like a cat, I'll settle my body down on the bed. Nicolette's face will light up.

Now it is not a dream, nor a daydream. I am really here, sitting on the plane. I look at my watch. It is twenty minutes to midnight. The plane swoops in a circle. I press my hot face against the cold pane.

Down there, sparkling lights. The lights of Firenze.

My ears are beginning to hurt.

THE BEGINNING

THREE
KINDS
OF
CONTENTS

CHRONOLOGY

(Horizontal Contents)

NARRATION

(Vertical Contents)

27.	49.	23.	18.	(6.)
24.	19.	25.	(1.)	(7.)
24.	(17.)	48.	(5.)	(8.)
24.	28.	36.	(7.)	(9.10.11.12.13.)
24.	28.	37.	(7.&18.&1.)	14.
24.	35.	2.	(7.)	18.
24.	(17.)	3.	(8.)	40.
29.	47.	4.	(9.)	40.&15.&12.
−1.	47.	32.	(10.)	41.
30.	31.	33.	(11.)	(17.)
0.	1.	5.	(12.&4.)	43.
15.	6.	34.	(13.)	44.
22.	15.	39.	18.	45.
20.	18.	38.	(1.)	42.
21.	(17.)	39.	(2.)	46.
18.	16.	16.	(3.)	∞.
50.	26.	(17.)	(5.)	27.

Total: 85 chapters.

STRUCTURE

(Cross-Contents)

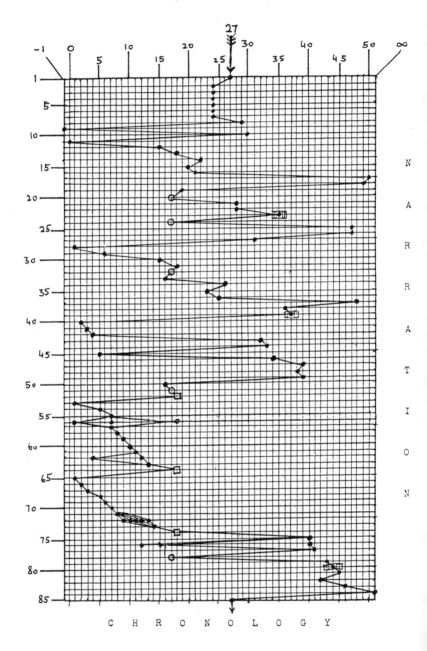

ROBERT ZEND (Budapest, 1929 – Toronto, 1985)

Robert Zend, poet, author, documentary producer and inveterate doodler, emigrated to Canada in 1956 following the Soviet invasion of Hungary. He received his undergraduate degree from the Péter Pázmány University in Budapest in 1953, and earned an M.A. in Italian literature from the University of Toronto in 1969.

Zend was a prolific writer in both English and Hungarian. His collections of poetry include *From Zero To One, Beyond Labels* and a series of *The Three Roberts* poetry readings with Robert Priest and Robert Sward. Some of his short stories, on the themes of dreams and time, were recently published in *Daymares. Arbormundi* and *My Friend Jerónimo* feature some of his visual work and concrete poetry. Foremost among his English-language publications, however, is the multi-genre creation of a miniature universe: *Oāb*.

Among the English-language journals that have published his works are *The Tamarack Review, Canadian Literature, Performing Arts, Chess Canada, Earth and You, The Toronto Star, Canadian Fiction Magazine* and *The Malahat Review*. The literary quarterly, *Exile*, has published excerpts from his longer visual works: *Oāb, A Bouquet to Bip, Limbo Like Me*, and *Typescapes: A Mystery Story*. He was a regular and enthusiastic contributor to *Rampike* and, in addition, his work has been featured in many English-language anthologies, among which are *Made in Canada, Volvox, The Sounds of Time, The Speaking Earth, To Say the Least, The Poets of Canada, In Praise of Hands, Colombo's Canadian Quotations, The Maple Laugh Forever, Lords of Winter and Love, Shoes and Shit—Stories for Pedestrians, Tesseracts* (Canada), *A Critical Ninth Assembly, Stellar 6: Science Fiction Stories, Peter's Quotations, The Writer and Human Rights* (U.S.) and *Blue Umbrellas* (Australia).

His work also appeared in numerous Hungarian-language publications, including *Hungarian Life, Mirror, Hungarian Panorama, Menora, Toronto Mirror, Literary Gazette* (Paris), *New Horizons* (Munich), *Atelier hongrois* (Paris), and *Szivárvány* (Chicago). He was included, as well, in László Kemenes-Géfin's *Anthology of Hungarian Poets Abroad* (Vienna), and a volume of his visual work, *Versek, képversek*, was published by Atelier hongrois in 1988. *Hazám törve kettővel*, based on journals kept during his return trips to

Hungary, was recently published in Canada. *Fából vaskarikatúrák,* a volume of parodies, has just been published in Hungary.

Zend gave poetry readings at the Eglinton Gallery, The Royal Ontario Museum, Harbourfront, The China Court Café, the University of Toronto, and in various cities throughout Canada. He participated in the Writer and Human Rights Conference in Toronto, 1981, the 6th and 7th Great Canadian Poetry Festival at Collingwood, 1981 and 1982, the David Bohm Symposium at Carleton University, 1983, and was writer-in-residence at Trent University, 1983.

Starting as a shipper with the Canadian Broadcasting Corporation in 1958, Zend rose through the ranks as a film librarian and film editor to become a radio producer. As a member of the CBC *Ideas* program team, he researched, wrote, directed and produced over one hundred radio programs featuring such notables as Northrop Frye, Glenn Gould, A.Y. Jackson, Norman McLaren, Marshall McLuhan, Harold Town, Isaac Asimov, Immanuel Velikovsky, Marcel Marceau, Andrei Voznesensky, Jorge Luis Borges, Princess Martha de Ruspoli, and the Dalai Lama. His series "The Lost Continent of Atlantis" was broadcast in the United States, Great Britain and Australia, as well as in Canada.

Zend's accomplishments in the visual arts include winning a prize in the International Photo Contest (Budapest 1968) and exhibiting his work in the International Craft Show at the Ontario Science Centre. His visual text creation, "Monpoem," was included in the 1984 retrospective of Spanish painter Manuel H. Mompó in Florence, Italy. An exhibition of his visual work was organised by art historian Oliver Botár, with the assistance of Tom Juranka, at the Metro Toronto Reference Library in 1986.